Calico

An Imprint of Magic Wagon
abdopublishing.com

· THE GRAVEYARD DIARIES ·

ZOMBIES REVISITED

by Baron Specter   illustrated by Robin Boyden

FOR MY NEPHEW, MAX—RB

abdopublishing.com

Published by Magic Wagon, a division of ABDO, PO Box 398166, Minneapolis, Minnesota 55439. Copyright © 2019 by Abdo Consulting Group, Inc. International copyrights reserved in all countries. No part of this book may be reproduced in any form without written permission from the publisher. Calico™ is a trademark and logo of Magic Wagon.

Printed in the United States of America, North Mankato, Minnesota.
052018
092018

 **THIS BOOK CONTAINS RECYCLED MATERIALS**

Written by Baron Specter
Illustrated by Robin Boyden
Edited by Bridget O'Brien
Art Directed by Christina Doffing

Library of Congress Control Number: 2018931812

Publisher's Cataloging-in-Publication Data

Names: Specter, Baron, author. | Boyden, Robin, illustrator.
Title: Zombies revisited / by Baron Specter; illustrated by Robin Boyden.
Description: Minneapolis, Minnesota : Magic Wagon, 2019. |
    Series: Graveyard diaries set 2; Book 9
Summary: Barry's usual walk through Marshfield Grove with his
    dog Lucy turns ominous when they encounter the ghost of Byron
    Mumford. He warns them of zombies in the graveyard, the same
    zombies Barry and his friends fought a few months ago. But after
    a zombie sneaks up on him, Barry wonders if he can trust Byron's
    word. He devises a plan with the Zombie Hunters to make the
    undead permanently dead.
Identifiers: ISBN 9781532131806 (lib.bdg.) | ISBN 9781532132209
    (ebook) | ISBN 9781532132407 (Read-to-me ebook)
Subjects: LCSH: Zombies--Juvenile fiction. | Haunted places--
    Juvenile fiction. | Ghost stories--Juvenile fiction. |
    Detective and mystery stories--Juvenile fiction.
Classification: DDC [FIC]--dc23

TABLE OF CONTENTS

Chapter 1: WHO'S WATCHING? 6

Chapter 2: GHOST CHATTER 17

Chapter 3: SET UP? 26

Chapter 4: A LONG NIGHT 36

Chapter 5: NO GOOD IDEAS 46

Chapter 6: SLIMY DEAD FLESH 57

Chapter 7: STILL DEAD? 69

Chapter 8: A SICKENING THUD 80

Chapter 9: IT'S ALL IN THE TIMING 89

Chapter 10: A ZOMBIE BURIAL 101

HUNTING ZOMBIES 110

ZOMBIE FACTS 111

ABOUT THE AUTHOR & ILLUSTRATOR 112

· CHAPTER 1 ·

WHO'S WATCHING?

Blood! Barry Bannon stepped carefully to avoid the dark red drops on the grassy path. Did the blood come from an injured animal? Or something worse?

"Maybe a hawk nabbed a chipmunk," Barry said. He turned to

his dog, Lucy. She sniffed at the blood and looked up.

"It's fresh," Barry said. "Must have happened a few minutes ago."

Barry and Lucy walked through Marshfield Grove Cemetery every day. They'd seen many things that were scarier than blood.

Ghosts were common here and in the town's other three cemeteries. Barry had seen them at night.

But the graveyard was peaceful during daylight. The sun wouldn't set for an hour yet.

Barry and his parents lived right on the edge of Marshfield Grove. Sometimes he'd sneak out to look for ghosts. He knew the hot spots.

He considered this his cemetery. His four friends also lived on the edges of graveyards. They formed a group they called the Zombie Hunters.

Barry and Lucy climbed the hill toward their favorite gravestone. Byron Mumford's stone was a large, granite rectangle.

It was much bigger than the surrounding stones. The stone said he'd died in 1887. The gravestone was surrounded by thick, hemlock trees.

When Barry was little, he called the spot Fort Mumford. He'd sled down the hill in winter. And in the summer, he'd lie in the gravestone's shade.

Today he wanted to write. He sat with his back against the stone. He took out his notebook.

Barry's Diary: Friday, September 9. 6:06 p.m.

Visiting Mumford. Was a hot day but it's cooling off now.

Peaceful evening. No trouble here in Marshfield Grove since that battle last

March. Something feels weird today though.

> Blood on the path.
> A sign of trouble?
> Things have been calm.
> Will this burst the bubble?

Something scuffled in the bushes.
Lucy raised her ears and growled.

"Just birds," Barry said. "Or a squirrel."

He felt sweat bead up on his forehead. He stared at the bushes. He was never nervous in the graveyard. But something wasn't right.

All seemed calm again. After a minute, Barry picked up his notebook.

I'll bet I've been in this graveyard 3,000 times. I've had some scary moments. A zombie battle last spring. A few surprise meetings with some angry ghosts.

I've always handled those well. So why do I feel uneasy now? The sun is still up. And there's no one else around here.

Lucy feels it, too. She's shaking a little. That's not like her.

Maybe we should get out of here, Barry thought. He shook his head. "Nothing's going to scare us out of our cemetery. Right Lucy?" She licked his face. Barry hugged her.

Even though the early evening was warm, Barry felt an icy breeze on his neck.

"What is that?" he asked. Lucy jumped. "It's okay, girl," Barry said, patting her back. She growled again and circled the gravestone.

Barry stood, too. Of all the eerie places in this cemetery, he'd never had trouble here. He'd never even seen a ghost nearby.

But something was going on now. The air tingled his skin.

"Maybe there's a thunderstorm on the way," Barry said.

The sky looked clear. If there was lightning in the distance, he might be feeling it. But he'd also hear the thunder, wouldn't he? He didn't.

Barry looked around. Nothing was moving. Nothing looked unusual. It was just a feeling.

"Who's watching us, Lucy?" he whispered. He was certain that something was.

Maybe a deer. They could stand perfectly still and never make a sound. And they blended in with the forest.

Barry let out a deep breath. He shoved his notebook into his pocket. He turned for home.

Right in his path was a misty gray ghost! An older man. He didn't look angry. But the air around him was cold.

"Are you Byron Mumford?" Barry asked.

The ghost nodded slowly. "Yes, I am. And something is wrong in my graveyard!"

· CHAPTER 2 ·

GHOST CHATTER

As the evening grew darker, Byron Mumford's ghost grew brighter. The air smelled like burned hot dogs.

Is somebody having a cookout? Or is that rotting flesh? Barry wondered.

"The evil is back," Mumford said.

"You?" Barry asked.

"Not me!" the ghost said. "The undead. They've awoken. And they're disturbing the peace of the cemetery."

"Zombies?" Barry and his friends had sent three zombies back to their graves last March. He was certain they'd finished them off. "Are they the same ones as last time?"

Mumford nodded. "They return from time to time. You think you can kill them, but you can't. They're already dead!

"All anyone can do is shut them down for a while. They always manage to come back. Sometimes it takes many years. Sometimes not."

Barry glanced down the hill. There was a pit on a slope above the river. A tangle of brush surrounded it.

That's where the zombies were buried. The Zombie Hunters had knocked them out and filled their mouths with salt. Salt killed zombies. Or at least it made them powerless for a bit.

"I've been visiting your grave for years," Barry said. "Why have I never seen you before?"

"I've been dead for over a century."

"I know," Barry said. "But here you are now. Talking to me."

Mumford swept his hand through the air, stopping to point at several gravestones. "What is the most common phrase on these stones?"

"Rest in peace," Barry replied.

"Yes. We rest until our peace is disturbed. Like right now."

"How are the zombies disturbing you?" Barry asked.

Mumford let out a sigh. Darkness had set in, but Barry could see him clearly. His face looked tired and old. "They disturb me by what they do to this peaceful place.

"They kill the birds and small animals. They eat their brains. When you are bound to one spot, as I am in death, the small creatures of nature bring great joy."

"They do it when we're alive, too," Barry said. "Lucy and I come here for nature as well. We listen to the birds, watch the squirrels and butterflies."

"And I watch you," Mumford said. "I've seen you grow up."

Barry had so many questions. He didn't know if they were polite to ask. But this was the best conversation he'd ever had with a ghost. "Do you talk to the other ghosts?"

"Not often," Mumford said. "Some ghosts are sharp-minded, as I am. But most are weary. Or they're stuck. They don't know they're dead. Some repeat the same things over and over. It's as if they left something undone when they were alive."

Barry lowered his voice. "But why are you still here?"

"Where else should I be?" the ghost responded. "I am at peace here. My periods of rest can last for years.

"I am not always aware of the passing of time. I like it that way. But lately my rest has been disturbed, as I said. The undead have made things unpleasant."

"Maybe we can help."

"You'll have to act quickly. The zombies are sluggish and slow. But they are gaining strength. The more brains they eat, the more alive they become."

The air turned stale. It smelled like dead fish. Barry felt a cold, slimy hand on his shoulder.

He turned and kicked at a zombie who had snuck up from behind. The zombie swung a fist at his head. Barry ducked and ran.

"Go, Lucy!" Barry dodged past a second zombie. Lucy ran ahead. Barry didn't look back. He could hear the zombies lumbering after him.

He sprinted through the dark cemetery. Down the hill. Along the river. Away from those zombies fast!

· CHAPTER 3 ·

SET UP?

Barry and Lucy left the cemetery at the farthest spot from home. They'd walk the streets instead of risking another zombie attack.

Barry always carried a leash in case they met another dog or a skunk. He almost never had to use it. But he snapped it onto Lucy's collar. He wasn't ready to go home.

They headed to their friend Jared's house. Jared lived on the edge of Woodland Cemetery. He was a member of the Zombie Hunters.

Barry was eager to tell him the news. Jared knew those zombies. They'd battled the same ones in March.

The one that grabbed Barry was short and had one eye. The other was huge, with strong shoulders. There had been a third zombie last time. Where was he?

Barry approached Jared's house. He spotted a single headlight coming toward him. Was there a motorcycle in Jared's yard?

"Hey!" Jared called. He shut off the engine of whatever he was riding.

"What are you doing?" Barry asked.

"I was mowing the lawn."

"In the dark?"

"It wasn't dark when I started," Jared said. "And I have a light. See?"

Barry could see that Jared had been riding a lawn tractor. "What do you need that for? I use a push mower."

"We have a quarter acre of lawn," Jared replied. "It's a big job."

Barry shook his head and laughed. "That's like using a steamroller to hammer a nail."

Jared shrugged. "What are you up to? You're all sweaty."

"I'll fill you in," Barry said. "Can you get us some water?"

Barry paced the driveway while Jared went to get drinks. Then they sat on the curb. Barry told him about the ghost and the zombies. "Sounds like Mumford is worried," Jared said.

"I'm not sure," Barry said. "He let the zombies sneak up on me. He had to know they were there. I think he was trying to help them get my brain."

"Why would he do that?" Jared asked.

"Who knows?" Barry said. "He acted all worried about the zombies 'disturbing his peace.' But he either wasn't paying attention or he wanted them to get me.

"They came this close to trapping me. I think he set me up. Maybe he's working with them." Barry finished his water and wiped his mouth.

"I'm all worked up," he said. "My heart is racing. My ears are ringing. All I can smell is those zombies."

"What do they smell like again?" Jared asked.

"Dead worms. Fish. Garbage." Barry let out another deep breath. He eyed the basketball rim above Jared's driveway. "Let's shoot some hoops. It'll help me calm down."

"I'll get the ball," Jared said. "We should alert Mitch, Amy, and Stan about this. We'll have a Zombie Hunters meeting tomorrow."

"Yeah," Barry said. "We need a strategy session in the morning. We need to act quickly. Tomorrow night."

Jared bounced the basketball to Barry. "One-on-one?" he asked.

Barry shook his head. "Nah. Just a shoot-around. I don't feel like competing. I just ran for my life, remember?"

He dribbled toward the basket. The ball hit a rough spot in the driveway and spun off to the side. Barry kicked at the spot. Some dusty concrete pebbles bounced away.

"Your driveway is in bad shape," Barry said. "Didn't you pave it just last year?"

Jared frowned. "My dad did it himself to save money. I helped. But we didn't really know what we were doing. The concrete was too watery. And we have six bags left over. Guess we didn't mix enough in. We probably laid it on too thin."

"Looks like it," Barry said. He swept his foot over the crumbly concrete again. "I guess it's better than nothing."

"Yeah, it was a heavy job," Jared said. "Not heavy enough, I guess. We'll probably have to re-do it next summer."

Barry scooped up the ball and shot at the basket. The ball fell cleanly through the hoop. Lucy chased after it as it rolled onto the grass.

"I should get her home," Barry said. "Let's meet at 10 a.m. You'll let the others know?"

"Sure."

Barry took the long way home. He loved Marshfield Grove Cemetery. But he didn't want to get close to it again tonight. Not until he was safely inside his own house.

· CHAPTER 4 ·

A LONG NIGHT

September 9. 9:48 p.m.

You can never really tell about people. Or ghosts. I've been playing by Mumford's grave since I was five. It always felt like a calm, safe place. Why would he turn on me now?

Barry stared out his bedroom window. He couldn't see Mumford's grave. It was on the other side of the cemetery.

Would the zombies make their way here? Probably not yet. They needed strength. Eating brains would do it.

We have to stop them, he thought.

Lucy was curled up on his bed. She never had trouble sleeping. Barry yawned, but knew he wouldn't sleep well. He tried to write another poem.

Byron Mumford, dead so long.
Weakened zombies, getting strong.
How I wish that I was wrong.
But I think they want to kill me.

I'll come up with a real rhyme. "Song" would fit, but it doesn't work.

How I wish they'd all be quiet.
But I think they want me dead.

Nope. Poems are hard! One more try, then I'm going to sleep.

How I wish it wasn't true.
But I think they'd kill me, too.

Not my best, but enough for now. I want to write a poem that ends with the word victory. (Finding a rhyme might be harder than defeating zombies!)

Barry's phone buzzed.

Jared had sent him a text. All set 4 tomorrow. 10 at bagel shop.

Barry wrote back. Everybody?

Jared: All in. U ok?

Barry: Shook up.

Jared: Hang in there. We got this.

Barry frowned. He wasn't so confident. Like last time?

Jared: Better. For real this time. We finish the job.

Barry looked out the window. Lightning flashed in the distance. Then he heard thunder. That might be a good sign.

The zombies would stay in their pit. Hunting wouldn't be good in a storm.

I don't want them gaining any more strength, he thought. *We need to stop them while they're weak.*

Jared sent another text. I have a question.

Barry ignored it and silenced his phone. He picked up his diary instead.

10:31 p.m.

What I don't get is why Mumford suddenly appeared. His explanation is full of holes. It's a peaceful place. So I can see why he'd be against the zombies.

But how could he not have known they were sneaking up on me? He was looking in that direction.

All those years and he'd never been visible before. But he says he's been watching me all this time. If that's true, why appear now? To distract me? So the zombies could get me?

I never did anything to bother him.
Always treated his grave with respect.
So I don't get it. He acted like he was
angry at the zombies.

Is that true or did he have me fooled?
It almost cost me my life!

Barry yawned deeper this time. He
shut off his light and got under the
covers. Then he got up and made sure
his window was locked.

Calm down, he told himself. *You're
safe*.

Lucy whined. "You okay, girl?" Barry
asked. But Lucy was just dreaming.
Probably about those zombies.

Barry got in bed. Soon he was asleep, dreaming about the same thing.

The zombies had him cornered, with his back to Mumford's grave. Six of them stepped closer. They blocked any path he had to escape.

Barry climbed onto the stone, grabbing hold of the cross. He tried to shake it loose to use it as a weapon. But it was attached to the stone.

Barry kicked at the nearest zombie. Another swung a hand at his legs. With a shaking rumble the stone began to churn.

The stone crashed to the ground. A flash of light cut through the air.

Barry sat up in bed, wide awake. Why was he still hearing rumbles?

The sky outside his window flickered with a bright light.

Lightning, Barry realized. *And thunder. No zombies.*

He checked his phone for the time. Not even midnight.

"Tomorrow better get here quick," he mumbled. "We need a plan. We have to send those zombies back to zombieland. Make them un-undead!"

· CHAPTER 5 ·

NO GOOD IDEAS

Barry got to the bagel shop early. He sat on the steps and waited for his friends. The town seemed quiet and peaceful. No one else knew about the zombies.

It's up to us, Barry thought. He took out his pad to make a few notes.

Saturday, September 10. 9:44 a.m.

Last night's conditions: Stormy. But the early evening was nice. Light breeze. Lots of small animals moving around. Good evening for zombies to hunt. Or for hunting zombies?

The morning was cool. Barry pulled up his sweatshirt hood. He slid aside as an older couple walked up the steps.

Mitch came zooming over on his skateboard.

"Any ideas?" Barry asked.

Mitch shook his head. "Nope. I thought we killed them last time with that salt. If that didn't work, we're lost."

"But it did work," Barry said. "A little. They were 'dead' for six months."

"And now they're back."

"Not all of them," Barry said. "There were only two zombies last night. Last time there were three. The other one may still be dead."

"True," Mitch said. "Or there might be more this time."

"Two is bad enough."

"I guess we'll find out," Mitch said. "I don't want to be the next person to die. Zombies want to eat human flesh and brains!"

"We have to finish them off before they can do that. We need a plan," Barry replied.

Mitch frowned. "I thought about it all night."

"And?"

"Nothing."

Amy, Stan, and Jared weren't much help either. But they all agreed to visit the cemetery that afternoon.

"Let's go in the shop," Jared said. "I'm starving."

"I want a brain sandwich," Stan said.

"Very funny." Barry ordered a raisin bagel. He'd skipped dinner after that brush with Mumford and the zombies. He hadn't even thought about food until now.

Everyone was stumped. But they agreed that they had to act quickly. They'd look for clues in the graveyard that afternoon. Maybe they'd get some ideas.

"Zombies usually aren't active in daylight," Jared said.

"We'll still need to be careful," Barry said. "I saw fresh blood in the early evening yesterday. They might have been hunting before sundown."

"That's a bad sign," Stan said. "If they're risking being out in daylight, they must be frantic for food."

"For brains," Jared said.

Barry set down his bagel. Suddenly he wasn't hungry. *I came close to being killed last night,* he thought. *Maybe this is too dangerous.*

The others seemed eager to fight. "Bring bats and clubs," Mitch said.

"We'll need to knock them out if they attack."

"And fill their mouths with salt again?" Amy asked. "Don't we need a different tactic?"

Barry nodded. But he had no idea what it might be.

"Didn't we learn anything from our last fight?" Mitch asked.

"We didn't have to learn anything." Barry shook his head. "We just had to kill them."

"It sounds awful, but we need to chop off their heads," Stan said.

"Gross," said Mitch.

"Dangerous!" added Jared.

"This whole thing is dangerous," Barry said. But he fought back his fear.

"That didn't stop us the last time we battled the zombies," he continued. "It hasn't stopped us with ghosts or vampires or werewolves. The Zombie Hunters have to be fearless."

"And we have to be smart," Amy said. "Fearless and stupid means injured or dead! I'll tell you what we learned. They're sneaky. They're powerful. And they'd kill us if they had the chance."

Barry let out his breath. He remembered the zombie's smell and the slimy skin.

He stared at his half-eaten bagel. Then he picked it up and tossed it in the trash. He couldn't eat another bite, even though his stomach rumbled.

Barry's Diary: Saturday, September 10. 4:45 p.m.

We're meeting in the cemetery in fifteen minutes. I have my hatchet and my hockey stick. A flashlight. A carton of salt.

It's not enough salt to kill a zombie. But it might slow one down. Give me enough time to knock it out.

I don't want to chop any heads off. It might be our only choice. I keep reminding myself that the zombies are already dead. And they want to kill us.

We're fighting the zombie threat
We'll do what we need to survive
This may be our hardest job yet
I hope I get back here alive!

· CHAPTER 6 ·

SLIMY DEAD FLESH

Barry's first goal was to see if the third zombie was active. Fighting two would be easier than three. He knew where they'd left the third zombie. In that pit with the other two.

"Stay close to me," Barry said to the Zombie Hunters. "And keep a close watch. If you see any sign of the zombies, yell!"

Barry worked his way down the steep hill. Brambles scratched his arms. Loose stones slid under his feet. He took out his flashlight and shined it in the hole.

The pit was about ten feet deep. Barry had been down there during his last zombie battle. He didn't ever want to go down there again.

But he needed to know what was down there now.

"All clear?" Barry yelled.

"All clear!" Mitch called from thirty yards away.

"No problems!" Amy shouted.

The light settled at the bottom of the hole. He saw a pile of small animals. Chipmunks. Squirrels. A rabbit. Most of the heads had been chewed off. Some looked freshly killed.

Then Barry saw what he'd been hoping for. Two rotten feet stuck out of a pile of dirt.

They were from the third zombie. That one hadn't moved since last March. Maybe he never would again.

"He's here!" Barry called. "Still dead!"

There was no answer.

"Mitch?" Barry yelled. "Amy?"

"Run, Barry!" It was Stan's voice. He sounded far away.

Barry leaped to his feet. The big zombie plodded down the hill toward him. Where was his one-eyed friend?

Barry scrambled down the other side of the hill. He had left his stuff with the others. All he had to defend himself with was the flashlight.

But he could definitely outrun a zombie.

His foot caught on a root, and Barry went down. The light rolled away. Within seconds, the zombie grabbed him with both hands.

"Let go!" Barry yelled, kicking at the zombie's legs. "Help!"

"We're coming!" called Amy. "The other one's chasing Mitch."

Barry gagged from the smell of the zombie's dead flesh. He twisted and kicked and punched at the slimy skin. The zombie held him tight.

The zombie roared. Disgusting yellow drool dripped from his mouth. He chomped at the air, trying to drive his teeth into Barry's neck. Barry squirmed. "Help!" he called again.

Thunk! Stan whacked the zombie across the back with a bat. The zombie loosened its grip. Barry dropped to his knees, trying to pull free. Then the zombie grabbed him harder.

Don't get bit, Barry told himself. The zombie chomped again. Saliva dripped onto Barry's face. But he stayed clear of the teeth.

Stan pounded the zombie again. Amy hit him with a hammer. The zombie seemed stunned. He let up, and Barry rolled on the ground.

Barry made it to his feet. He heard his sweatshirt rip as the zombie swiped him. But finally he was free.

Barry raced up the slope behind Amy and Stan. The zombie did not follow.

At the top of the hill, Barry looked back. The zombie was kneeling at the pit. The pounding had stunned him.

The other zombie walked over. They crawled into the pit.

Barry's heart was pounding.

"Did he bite you?" Amy asked.

Barry shook his head. "So close. I was nearly a dead man."

"So much for them only striking at night," Stan said.

"I think that's only in the movies," Amy said. "In real life, they can get you any time."

Barry kept looking back as they walked. He knew they could outrun the zombies. But that big zombie was strong. "I never would have escaped without your help," he said.

What had happened to Mitch and Jared? Had the other zombie hurt them? Barry yelled their names. Jared called back. He was down near the entrance.

"Mitch is hurt," Jared said as they approached.

"Did the zombie get him?" Barry asked.

Jared shook his head. "We outran him easily," he said. "But Mitch fell and turned his ankle."

"It hurts," Mitch said. "I need to get some ice on it to stop the swelling." He put one arm around Stan's shoulders and the other around Amy's.

"We'll take him home," Amy said. "I think that's enough zombie hunting for one day. Otherwise we'll all wind up hurt."

"Or worse," Stan said. "I agree. Let's rethink this and meet again tomorrow."

Barry was still shaking from his fight. He wiped his hands on his torn sweatshirt, smearing zombie drool on it. "Okay," he said softly.

Stan, Amy, and Mitch hobbled off toward Mitch's house. Jared closed the gate. "Enough for today?" he asked Barry.

"Not even close," Barry replied. "Let's go to your house. I think I know how to solve this!"

· CHAPTER 7 ·

STILL DEAD?

Saturday, September 10. 5:51 p.m.

Grossest thing ever! I have slime and drool all over me. I guess that's better than being eaten.

Jared's getting some towels for me in the house. But what I really want is his lawn tractor. Everything else we need to beat the zombies is right here in Jared's garage.

"I told my parents you fell in the mud." Jared handed Barry some wet paper towels. "So what's your big idea?"

"It's tricky," Barry said, wiping his arms and his neck. "These zombies are hard to kill. So we have to trap them. Make it so they can't be active even if they never die."

"That's easier said than done," Jared replied. "And without Mitch, we're down to four of us."

"We can do it alone," Barry said. "This needs to be finished now. I don't think Stan or Amy want anything to do with it tonight. You heard them."

Jared leaned against the garage wall and folded his arms. "I'm not so sure I want a part of this either. Not tonight anyway."

"Tonight's perfect," Barry said. "One of the zombies is hurt. That gives us an advantage. But that might not last long."

Jared rolled his eyes. "So what do we do?"

"Mow the lawn."

"I did it yesterday."

Barry leaned closer and lowered his voice. "Make it seem like you're finishing the lawn. Then we'll head for the cemetery."

"On the tractor?"

"Yeah."

"I don't get it," Jared said. He scratched his head. "That tractor is slow. There's no way it could run down a zombie."

"You'll see. It has a cart, right?"

"Yeah," Jared replied. He pointed to the cart in the corner of the garage. "It attaches easily."

"Start the tractor. Then swing by the side of the garage," Barry said. "I'll load up the cart."

"With what?"

"Those," Barry said with a grin. He pointed to the leftover bags of concrete.

The bags weighed thirty pounds apiece. Barry struggled to load them all. They filled the cart. He carefully set two trash cans and a bucket on top.

His hockey stick and Jared's bat were still in the graveyard.

"Are we building the zombies a house?" Jared asked. He pulled up in the tractor. "A comfy concrete home?"

"You could say that," Barry replied. "A home forever, I hope. One they can't break out of."

The concrete made the tractor move at a snail's pace. But soon they were crossing the neighbors' lawn.

The tractor left a wide path of cut grass. "Can't you raise the cutter?" Barry walked alongside the tractor.

Jared looked back at the oddly cut grass. "I forgot."

When they reached the cemetery, Barry pointed to the river. It wound around the edge of the graveyard. And it passed near the slope where the zombies stayed.

"We'll hide the tractor by the river," he said. "Then we'll check the pit."

"I still don't get it," Jared said. But he shut off the tractor and followed Barry up the hill.

Barry's flashlight was bright yellow. He found it easily about twenty feet below the pit. He motioned to Jared to stay quiet. Then they stepped carefully up the slope.

Barry shined the light into the pit. He found the feet sticking out of the dirt.

"That one's still dead," he mouthed, not making any sound.

He pointed to the nearby, broken up dirt piles. The other zombies had pushed free of the dirt when they awoke.

Barry walked away from the pit. He waved for Jared to follow. "The dirt wasn't enough to hold them. The concrete will do it."

Jared let out a short breath. "All we have to do is get them to lie still. Then we mix the concrete, pour it down the pit onto them, and wait for it to dry. Good luck with that."

"Do you have a better idea?"

Jared stared at the pit. He shook his head. "Let's get my bat. Maybe we can ambush them as they come out."

"That's what I'm counting on." Barry laughed. "What could go wrong?"

Jared laughed softly, too. "Let's see. We could get bit. Killed. Have our heads ripped off. You're right. It'll be easy."

Barry shook his head. "I never said that. But I don't see any other choice. If we don't act tonight, those zombies will get stronger. There will be no stopping them after that."

· CHAPTER 8 ·

A SICKENING THUD

Barry's Diary: Saturday, September 10. 6:57 p.m.

Waiting for dark. We can't mix the concrete yet because it dries quickly. But we've filled one trash barrel with river water. The other barrel is filled with the dry mix.

Had to do it on the cart because it's too heavy to lift. Hoping we can tip it into the pit after its mixed. But we have work to do first.

"I'll text Stan," Jared said. "Maybe he'll be willing to help."

"Can't hurt," Barry said. "Say we'll be by the pit in five minutes."

He hoped they could knock the zombies out as they climbed from the hole. A few whacks would do it.

But he wasn't sure it would work. They'd have to stay quiet. And hope the zombies didn't figure out they were waiting.

Barry took a deep breath. He'd kept Lucy out of the graveyard since yesterday. He was afraid the zombies would get her. He just wanted things to be normal again.

"Let's go," Barry said. They'd already collected their weapons.

"I feel like I'm marching off to war," Jared said. He raised his baseball bat.

"We are," Barry said, swinging his hockey stick. He started climbing the slope. *Be quiet*, he thought. *Sneak up*.

Jared's phone buzzed. "Stan's on his way."

"Good," Barry said. "But turn the phone off. I don't want it buzzing and tipping off the zombies."

The boys settled down on opposite sides of the pit. Barry's hands were sweating. The sun had set. Those hungry zombies should be climbing out soon.

Barry heard a grunt. Something was moving in the pit. He tightened his grip on the hockey stick. Soon a huge hand reached out of the hole. Then another.

The boys stood. Barry looked across at Jared. He saw the fear in his eyes. But Jared had his bat pulled back, ready to take a mighty swing.

The zombie lifted his head and shoulders from the hole. Both boys swung hard.

THUNK! WHAM!

Barry felt the sickening thud as his stick met the zombie's head. The zombie let out a groan. It fell back into the pit, landing with a crash.

Barry backed away, staring at the pit. Jared's eyes were wide. "Yow," he said. "I never hit anything harder in my life."

Barry was shaking. He shut his eyes for a second.

Footsteps behind him made him jump. "It's me." Stan hurried up to them.

"One down," Jared said, nodding toward the pit. "One to go."

"Which one did you get?"

"The big one, I think," Barry said. "Go see for yourself."

"Is the short one still down there?" Stan asked.

"I assume so. Be careful."

Barry and Jared stayed back as Stan walked to the pit. He kneeled at the top. He shined his light into the hole.

"You got the big one," Stan said. "He's out cold." Stan leaned into the pit. He looked around with his light.

"Don't fall in!" Barry said. "Get back here with us."

Stan took a step away from the pit. His eyebrows were raised. He waved for Barry to come closer. "We've got a problem," he said. "I don't see the other zombie."

"Mr. One-Eye? He's probably hiding down there," Barry said. "He'll come up to hunt. Then we'll whack him like we did the big one."

"No," Stan said. "You don't understand. The third zombie isn't down there either!"

"The dead one?"

"They're all dead!" Stan said.

"You know what I mean," Barry replied. "The third one. The one that hadn't woke up."

"That one," Stan said. His eyes opened wide and he pointed. "He's awake now. And he's right behind you. Look out!"

· CHAPTER 9 ·

IT'S ALL IN THE TIMING

The third zombie had green skin and sharp fingernails. He swiped at Barry and growled. Barry hit him with his hockey stick and leaped away.

The zombie dropped to his knees. He stared at the boys. Barry stepped back.

"He's got company," Jared said, pointing to the pit. The one-eyed zombie was crawling out.

"Run!" Barry said. He lowered his voice to a whisper. "I have an idea."

They reached the top of the hill. Barry had them stop by Byron Mumford's gravestone. The two zombies were following them.

"Those two are less of a problem than the big one," Barry said. "They're much slower and dumber. I think we can trick them. And finally get this over with."

"What's the plan?" Jared asked.

"Let them chase you," Barry said. "But split up. We want one of them chasing each of you. Lead them to the pit. I'll be waiting there."

"For what?" Stan asked.

"As bait." Barry tapped his stick on the stone. Then he handed it to Jared. Barry smacked his fists together. "If we time it right . . ."

The zombies lunged toward them. Each boy ran in a different direction.

Barry reached the pit. The big zombie hadn't moved. His eyes were open in a dead stare. Bloody slime dripped from his mouth. "Stay there," Barry said. "And stay dead!"

Jared and Stan were making a lot of noise. They were faster than the zombies, but wanted them to keep chasing. Barry kept his flashlight on. They needed to know where to go.

Jared ran close to the pit, but Stan wasn't there. "Circle back!" Barry called.

As Stan raced into view, Barry waved his arms. He yelled and caught the attention of both zombies.

They stopped chasing Stan and Jared. The zombies turned to Barry. They ran at him as fast as they could.

Barry leaped clear as the zombies dived for him. With a solid *CLUNK*, they smashed their heads. They dropped heavily into the pit.

Barry spun in the air. His right foot slipped on the edge of the pit. His left foot felt nothing. Down he went, right on top of the zombies!

Ooof! Barry lost his breath. He felt like he'd been punched twenty times. "Help!" he called.

"We'll get you," Stan yelled from above.

Stan's flashlight shone down on him. Barry could see that the zombies were knocked out. He stood up carefully, testing himself for broken bones. Everything seemed okay.

"Drop the bat to me," Barry said. He gave the zombies a whack to the head. He wanted to make sure.

Stan and Jared reached down, and Barry reached up. They pulled him out of the pit as he struggled to plant his feet.

"Now we finish the job," Barry said. "But we have to hurry. Those zombies can take a pounding and bounce back. If they wake up, we'll have to start over. And I'm tired of this!"

They hurried to the lawn tractor. Jared hopped on to drive. The wheels spun and the engine groaned. But the tractor wouldn't move.

The added weight from the concrete was too much. The tractor couldn't climb the hill.

"Push," Jared said. Barry and Stan found a safe spot and shoved. The tractor moved a couple of inches, then stopped.

"Push harder!" Jared said. But the boys were pushing as hard as they could.

Suddenly, the tractor began to move. Barry glanced behind them.

He saw Byron Mumford's ghost pushing the cart. Several other ghosts

joined him. They squeezed around the cart to help.

"You're helping us?" Barry asked, his eyes wide.

"Why wouldn't we?" Mumford replied. "We're going to stop those zombies forever. I meant what I told you last night."

Barry smiled. He had misjudged Mumford. "I was afraid you were trying to help them," he said. "When they snuck up on me."

"They fooled me, too," Mumford said. "I want peaceful presences in this cemetery. Like you and your dog. Not zombies!"

At the top of the hill, they mixed the concrete with the water. The barrels were heavy. But the ghosts helped dump the mixture into the pit. They covered the zombies in slimy, wet concrete.

"That will start to harden right away," Jared explained. "By morning it will be like they're buried in rock. And we mixed it right this time. No more crumbly stuff like my driveway!"

Barry wiped his forehead with his sleeve. "Let's hope it works," he said. "I don't ever want to battle those zombies again. Twice is more than enough!"

· CHAPTER 10 ·

A ZOMBIE BURIAL

Saturday, September 10. 11:58 p.m.

Every bone in my body aches from that fall. And from pushing the heavy tractor. But it was worth it.

Lucy is curled up by my feet. She's probably dreaming about running through the graveyard. We'll spend the day out there tomorrow.

It's ours again. Safe.

The worst things that I've ever
smelled
Are zombie skin and breath
They smell like puke and rot and slime
And never-ending death.

The Zombie Hunters gathered by the cemetery entrance early the next morning. Barry was the only one that had brought a shovel. He was pretty sure the concrete had worked.

But Barry figured some extra dirt might help, too. And it would make things look neater. The pit was too deep for them to fill with dirt entirely.

Mitch was on crutches, but he moved quickly. "Sprained ankle," he explained. "Should be better in a week."

Lucy ran ahead, straight toward the pit. Barry whistled for her to come back.

"Just in case," he said. "Let's make sure those zombies are dead, dead, dead."

The concrete was bumpy and uneven. But parts of the three

zombies were sticking out. They weren't moving.

Barry dropped carefully into the pit. He tapped the pile with his shovel. *Tick-pock*. It was solid.

Barry used the shovel to pile dirt on the concrete. He smoothed it out so none of the concrete or zombies were visible. Then he climbed out of the pit.

The other Zombie Hunters had gathered several branches from the hemlock trees. They hid the pit's entrance in branches. Lucy stayed close to Barry as they worked.

"Let those zombies rot down there forever," Barry said. "I've seen all I want of them."

"We brought some bagels," Stan said. He held up a paper bag. "Think you could maybe finish one today, Barry?"

Barry grinned. "I could eat three or four."

The morning was warm and sunny. Autumn would arrive soon, but it was still summer.

Barry took the Zombie Hunters back to Byron Mumford's grave. They sat in the shade to eat the bagels.

"Quite a year we've had so far," Barry said softly. "Marshfield is one spooky town. Zombies, ghosts, you name it."

"By the way," Stan said with a laugh. "You have dirt all over your face, dude."

"And my clothes," Barry said. "Who cares? It's all part of battling evil."

Barry closed his eyes and spread out on the grass. "I could sleep all day," he said. "Hardly rested at all the past two nights."

The others left for home. Only Barry and Lucy remained. Barry enjoyed the sun on his face for another hour. Lucy sniffed every inch of ground near the grave.

"It's all good now, Lucy," Barry said. He climbed to his feet and patted Mumford's gravestone.

"We'll be back every day," he said. "Rest in peace, Mr. Mumford. But don't sleep forever. We'll look forward to seeing you now and then."

HUNTING ZOMBIES

·TIPS FROM BARRY BANNON·

Step 1: LOOK FOR PILES OF DEAD ANIMALS, LIKE RABBITS AND CHIPMUNKS. ZOMBIES CHEW THEIR HEADS OFF TO EAT THEIR BRAINS.

Step 2: ALWAYS BE AWARE IF YOU SUSPECT ZOMBIES ARE NEAR. LISTEN FOR STRANGE SOUNDS. WATCH FOR CREEPY MOVEMENTS. SNIFF FOR TERRIBLE SMELLS.

Step 3: ZOMBIES CAN SNEAK UP ON YOU, SO HUNT THEM WITH A FRIEND. THAT WAY YOU CAN WATCH EACH OTHER`S BACKS.

Step 4: CARRY A FLASHLIGHT. SINCE YOU`LL BE HUNTING MOSTLY AT NIGHT, YOU NEED TO BE ABLE TO SEE.

Step 5: CEMETERIES ARE GREAT PLACES TO HUNT. BUT YOU MIGHT RUN INTO GHOSTS IN A GRAVEYARD, TOO. THE GHOSTS MIGHT HAVE SOME ADVICE FOR YOU.

ZOMBIE FACTS

·FROM BARRY BANNON·

#1: ZOMBIES EAT BRAINS TO GIVE THEMSELVES STRENGTH.

#2: ZOMBIES SMELL LIKE ROTTEN MEAT.

#3: ZOMBIES AREN'T ACTIVE DURING THE DAY UNLESS THEY'RE VERY HUNGRY.

#4: ZOMBIES ARE HARD TO KILL. SOMETIMES THEY COME BACK AFTER MANY YEARS.

#5: SALT CAN WEAKEN ZOMBIES IF YOU CAN GET THEM TO EAT A LOT OF IT.

#6: YOU CAN KNOCK OUT A ZOMBIE BY HITTING IT IN THE HEAD, BUT THAT PROBABLY WON'T KILL IT.

#7: ZOMBIES ARE MUCH STRONGER THAN LIVE PEOPLE.

#8: ZOMBIES DROOL!

ABOUT THE AUTHOR

BARON SPECTER IS THE PEN NAME OF RICH WALLACE, WHO HAS WRITTEN DOZENS OF BOOKS FOR KIDS. HIS LATEST BOOKS INCLUDE THE KICKERS SOCCER SERIES AND A NORTH POLE ADVENTURE CALLED *BOUND BY ICE*.

ABOUT THE ILLUSTRATOR

ROBIN BOYDEN IS AN ILLUSTRATOR BASED IN THE UK. HE HAS ILLUSTRATED MANY MAGAZINE EDITORIALS AS WELL AS NUMEROUS BOOKS FOR CHILDREN, INCLUDING THE SKATE MONKEY SERIES AND THE LATEST EDITIONS OF THE DEMON HEADMASTER. HIS FAVOURITE THINGS TO DRAW ARE BEARS AND CREEPY TREES.